Baby Shark!

Illustrated by Mike Jackson

 A GOLDEN BOOK • NEW YORK

Copyright © 2019 by Penguin Random House LLC. All rights reserved. Published in the United States by Golden
Books, an imprint of Random House Children's Books, a division of Penguin Random House LLC, 1745 Broadway,
New York, NY 10019. Golden Books, A Golden Book, A Little Golden Book, the G colophon, and the
distinctive gold spine are registered trademarks of Penguin Random House LLC.
rhcbooks.com
Educators and librarians, for a variety of teaching tools, visit us at
RHTeachersLibrarians.com
Library of Congress Control Number available upon request.
ISBN 978-0-593-12509-0 (trade) — ISBN 978-0-593-12510-6 (ebook)
Printed in the United States of America
10 9 8 7 6 5 4 3 2 1

Who will we find deep in the sea?

Why it's …

Baby Shark, doo doo doo doo doo doo.
Baby Shark, doo doo doo doo doo doo.
Baby Shark, DOO DOO DOO DOO DO

Mommy Shark, doo doo doo doo doo doo.
Mommy Shark, doo doo doo doo doo doo.
Mommy Shark, doo doo doo doo doo doo.

Mommy Shark!

Daddy Shark, doo doo doo doo doo doo.
Daddy Shark, doo doo doo doo doo doo.
Daddy Shark, doo doo doo doo doo doo.

Daddy Shark!

Grandma Shark, doo doo doo doo doo doo.
Grandma Shark, doo doo doo doo doo doo.
Grandma Shark, doo doo doo doo doo doo.

Grandma Shark!

Grandpa Shark, doo doo doo doo doo doo.
Grandpa Shark, doo doo doo doo doo doo.
Grandpa Shark, doo doo doo doo doo doo.

Swim around, doo doo doo doo doo doo.

Swim around, doo doo doo doo doo doo.

Swim around, DOO DOO DOO

Meet new friends, doo doo doo doo doo doo.
Meet new friends, doo doo doo doo doo doo.
Meet new friends, doo doo doo doo doo doo.

Meet new friends!

Have some fun, doo doo doo doo doo doo.
Have some fun, doo doo doo doo doo doo.
Have some fun, doo doo doo doo doo doo.

Have some fun!

Time to go, doo doo doo doo doo doo.
Time to go, doo doo doo doo doo doo.
Time to go, doo doo doo doo doo doo.

Time to go!

Home, sweet home, doo doo doo doo doo doo.
Home, sweet home, doo doo doo doo doo doo.
Home, sweet home, doo doo doo doo doo doo.

Home, sweet home!

HOME,
SWEET
HOME

Baby Shark!